THE MINER
STORIES
BOOK TWO

THE CONSPIRACY: The MINER BOOK 2

S.E. McKenzie

DEDICATION
To the miners everywhere who should have been safer.

CONTENTS

Chapter 1

Beginning of In-Reach entry, LOG #6:
by Christina Watson
(Accounting Assistant to Alex Coaltonstone).

December 25ᵗʰ 2030, around 6:00 p.m.

I am sitting here alone in my office. The waiting is torture.

Doctor Knight believes that this private journaling is very important and will help me to maintain some positivity while creating ownership of my self-identity. But she hasn't told me whether I am pregnant or not and she hasn't really told me the effect the pit atmosphere will have on Ginger's lung condition. I think he has something worse than asthma.

I was assigned a new job with a substantial raise today. James Coaltonstone dropped in my new assignment. I found out on the internet that Coaltonstone is giving the miners low interest loans so when this is all over they will owe Coaltonstone. He always finds a way to get ahead, no matter what. So my new assignment is to proof read his manuscript, "The Blessing: Black Diamonds." At first I thought he was joking and that he was going to give me updates concerning Ginger's rescue but he told me there is nothing to tell.

I can't imagine my life without Ginger. I really need him back. He has been stuck down there since Sunday and it is now Wednesday, Christmas day. It was wonderful to talk to him. The communication system worked without a hitch, thanks to Ginger's grandfather. It is easy enough to forget how much danger Ginger is still. I wish there were more people, than just Ginger's grandfather, willing to take a chance.

There are lots of people on both sides of the security fence coming and going. People are waving signs demanding that Ginger is rescued no matter the cost. Other signs being waved more aggressively are demanding the inclusion of the Exclusion League's policies. As I write, militia men and cadets are building a new wall, around the security fence between the public and Coaltonstone Mines' administration building. I feel like I am on the wrong side of the fence.

There are thousands of people standing together, some still in their mining clothes, complete with helmets and lights waiting for Ginger to ascend from Mine Five.

There are nuns, priests and pastors; I think I see a travelling rabbi too. Most of these people must be out of town since I have never seen them before except those waving vote for A.B. Peel placards. Most of them are here to support Ginger I hope.

End of In-Reach entry, LOG #6 by Christina Watson (Accounting Assistant to Alex Coaltonstone).

Chapter 2

December 25th 2030, around 6:15 p.m.

"Good Evening and welcome to Black Times. This is Dianne Black broadcasting live from Pitville Mine Disaster of 2030, on Christmas Day, which is also local hero; Ginger Goodwin's birthday. Unfortunately, Ginger Goodwin is still trapped 1,200 feet below the surface, as we speak.

Mr. Goodwin's location was discovered only after hours of PPZ's News Team's tireless investigative journalistic effort.

My moles tell me that all Coaltonstone Mine Five employees will be eligible for loan interest loans. Considering how high interests are at present, loans below market should be wonderful news for the miners. These loans will help the miners and their dependants subsist during the time the mine is closed.

At this time, we cannot stress how much, we at PPZ wish Mr. Goodwin a speedy rescue.

Ginger Goodwin's beautiful partner, Christina Watson communicated with her beau for a short time earlier this afternoon. The first explosion in Mine Five occurred at 5:20 a.m., Sunday morning, and many at PPZ are asking why didn't G.O.D.'s representatives facilitate communications with Ginger in a timelier manner?

According to Mr. Goodwin, the emergency telemagnetic radio, located in Safety Chamber in section E, has been in working order. The equipment survived the explosion which occurred in Section C partly due to design, and partly due to luck, according to our moles.

Now let us see if the beautiful Christina Watson will share a few words with us. As you can see the office building housing Coaltonstone Mines is luxurious. This long hall which leads to Christina's office is decorated with the usual Christmas fair including tinsel and lights.

"Hello Christina Watson."

"My God Dianne, you scared me, I was just writing my personal journal, I wasn't expecting you, are we live?"

"Yes we are! We have so much to celebrate; just one miracle after another. Ginger being found in one piece and a little one on the way. We, my viewers and I, are here with you. We know how hard this has been for you, especially with you expecting and all."

"How did you know I was pregnant? I don't even know yet. I mean I haven't talked to my doctor about my results yet."

"Well what do you want to know? It looks like you are going to have a boy and he is a healthy looking 21 week old fetus. He is adorable."

"You actually have a picture and I haven't even been told yet? How does that happen?"

"Christina, you know better to question how resourceful we are at PPZ. It is my job to know everything. We, and me in particularly, never reveal our sources. How was your visit with Pitville's hero?"

"The visit wasn't long enough. I wish they could find a way to get him out of there. I am so frightened for him, for me, for our little boy," Christina said as she struggled not to cry.

"You Know Christina, we all admire your courage, strength and sincerity."

"Thank you. I must say I am feeling overwhelmed. I have been waiting for news about Ginger and about my own condition, and I had no idea you could find out about such matters before me."

"I can't reveal my source but I can say one thing about the atmosphere on this side of the Security Fence, which is now being referred to as a wall. There is one atmosphere on the public side of the wall and another atmosphere on the private side. Right now everyone's movements are being watched by John Bell and his security staff but that is nothing new, my moles tell me."

"I was told that I would be better off not leaving the Admin Building until this horrible situation is resolved, but nothing seems to be happening. I must say that the military presence around here scares me, partly because I have never been around so people with so many guns. And they all seem to be lining up around the wall. I don't get why they are even building a wall. I guess I will just have to hang out in my office and wait."

"I just want to remind our audience that it is alleged that Ginger Goodwin wrote forty nine reports in forty seven days, complete with air quality measurements and photographs and every single report which we have in our possession, was ignored. Can you comment on this situation Christina?"

"Not really. I don't know how you got hold of those documents any more than I can figure out how you got hold of my medical records. I doubt very much Ginger has anything to do with it at all. If anything I think Ginger is being set up at a time when he is the most helpless."

"So you believe that Ginger Goodwin is not Deep Coal? Tell me why."

"I never heard of Deep Coal until PPZ discovered him. I have seen no real evidence that Ginger Goodwin, my Ginger has intentionally revealed any privileged Mine information. Ginger has been trapped in Mine Five since Sunday and he needs rescuing. I and my son Mathew need Ginger alive and by our sides."

"We all respect and admire Ginger Goodwin for his selfless action which saved Mine Five's morning crew on Sunday. And according to my sources, Deep Coal is thrilled that you are expecting a little boy sometime in late May or early June."

"Everyone seems to know all about my condition except me. I don't see how I can possibly officially be pregnant before my pregnancy is confirmed by my physician."

"Now, it is I who has an important question, and I certainly do judge. Do you believe that Ginger Goodwin is Deep Coal?"

"Of course I don't believe that? How could he be? He has been trapped in that mine since early Sunday morning. It has been three days that he has been down there. No one ever heard of Deep Coal until after he was trapped. I am grateful that PPZ was able to locate Ginger, but he is still in terrible danger. Did your source reveal Ginger's lung condition to you? He has been officially diagnosed with asthma but I think he has something more than that. He is trapped 1,200 feet under the ground and no one seems to be doing anything to get him out of there."

"Are you angry Christina?"

"Of course I am angry. I wish someone would rescue Ginger before another disaster strikes. This rain is scaring me. The smoke coming out of the sidewalk terrifies me. So many terrible things are happening and they are happening all at once.

"Well the weather conditions are certainly getting worse but reporting it is not my job."

"I know. Soon we will be under another water boil advisory," Christina said. "The rain will make the acid conditions in the mine worse, as in big time."

"What I meant, Christina, was that the weather report is separate from this report."

"Well that is stupid. The weather affects the safety of the mine."

"I thought you would be grateful that PPZ found Ginger.

"Of course I am grateful. Finding Ginger is the first step, and it shouldn't have been so hard. If he had been someone more important, like James Coaltonstone, I am sure he would have been found sooner. I hate waiting for the rescue to start. Everyone is talking and no one is doing anything."

"Talk about talking, I heard that you had a visit with Ginger. How is he doing? How is his lung condition?"

"Talking to Ginger this afternoon seemed surreal. He was so trapped down there you wouldn't believe it. Everything is so confusing. The militias are all over town, either working to expand the security fence or they are just staring at whoever they please, but no one except Ginger's grandfather seems to be doing anything to help actually rescue him."

"What do you mean exactly? I am sure that the rescue teams are doing their best. You must realize Christina that this situation is very complicated."

"Well the militias seem to be more organized and active than the rescue team. They had their guns strapped to their backs and were working on different parts of the security fence and now it looks like a wall in some parts. Everywhere I look, there are armed people in militia uniforms either looking out over the wall, or working on expanding the fence into a wall."

"Christina, I am sure they know what they are doing."

"What are they doing? I have heard nothing and I wish someone would at least tell me what they are actually doing. I hope they can pull him up to the surface without a lot of delay. They are going to send things down to him to improve communications and to make him more comfortable. They are sending things down to him in a tube through the air ventilation which is too narrow and too dangerous to expand into an escape shaft."

"Have you heard anything from G.O.D.?

"No nothing." Christina replied.

"The Government's Official Directors' office hasn't returned our calls either," Dianne said as she could see Jackson mouth out the word 'CUT'.

"While we were talking, Ginger was coughing so hard that I fear if he doesn't get out of there soon the damage to his lungs could be irreversible."

"I am sure everyone is doing the best they can. I am sure he is thrilled to be expecting a little one."

"He is. I think his grandfather told him. His grandfather told me that he heard I was expecting from the Old Boys Club. I find the whole thing rather strange since I haven't even received my results yet, or talked with my family doctor concerning my condition. I am glad Ginger's grandfather is here, and I am glad Ginger's grandfather is so rich, maybe now Ginger too will be too rich to ignore.

Chapter 3

December 25th 2030, around 6:30 p.m.

"Before we begin this meeting, I would like to apologize for interrupting everyone's Christmas day celebrations and I would like to introduce to you Jethro and Bill, who will be assisting John Bell with security," Mayor Stern said while Jethro and Bill waved while trying to maintain a pleasant manner in a very unpleasant situation.

"Everyone's Christmas has been shot this year. I can't remember a worse Christmas," James Coaltonstone said.

"That lowlife bar deal has finally gone through, so Pitville is now the proud owner of the Thirsty Pit'.

"Why?' Susan Jones asked.

"Because no one else wanted to buy it, and it has been under court ordered foreclosure for some time. So the plan is to tear it down and widen the roads, and bring in more coal trucks and send out more coal," Mayor Stern explained.

"How can anyone think of celebrating Christmas while Ginger is still trapped in the pit?" Susan asked as she looked around the room.

"What else could go wrong?" Don Bell asked while staring at his com-phone

"Well, I had my car stolen when I ran into Starbucks this morning," Mayor Stern grumbled.

"How did that happen?" Don Bell asked.

"We know how it happened. We are letting these strangers from outside take control over our way of life. We need to be more vigilante, We need those lazy cadets to work faster so that wall I ordered can start protecting us by keeping those people out of our world." John Bell said as he started to add more items to his list of things he wanted to control.

"Are you joking?" Susan asked.

"Why would I be?" John replied.

"I suppose it was partly my fault. I left the car running as I rushed in to Starbucks to get a quick coffee," Mayor Stern admitted.

"We used to always leave our doors open and cars running," James Coaltonstone said.

"It is a miracle that Ginger survived the explosion. We should be very thankful that Ginger was found alive by the Minese," Susan said. "I have updated all of my notes. I was referring to Ginger Goodwin in the past tense, which would now be incorrect since he is very much alive which I suppose makes this a very miraculous Christmas." Susan glanced around the room in her usual cheerful manner. "I have a question. Why can I hear and feel heavy freight coming in and going out when all of our shipments are officially cancelled due to the explosion in Mine Five?"

"Susan, what did we say about talking?"

"I am sorry sir, but if I can't communicate, my notes won't be a true record of what is being said in our meeting."

"Susan, please," Mayor Stern said as he stared at Susan.

"Okay, what should we discuss first?" Mayor Stern asked.

"We now know that our two new enforcer bots are with Ginger, so I have hired these two new detectives sir as replacements. I also suggest that we discuss implementation of a pass system, so that anyone who is moving about will be obligated to explain themselves, that way the strangers will know that they are being watched," John Bell said as he looked at his brother who was staring at him in disbelief.

"That Ginger seems to find a way to mess up my plans. Those bots were meant to be for security not to be data banks. Those bots are the state of the art bot-drones."

"Ginger must have assumed that the bots waiting in my office were the bots that he had been requesting for years. I had them sitting in my office, since John's office space was being used for something secret," Don Bell explained.

"Don, I was having a meeting with Bill and Jethro and we were discussing the feasibility of implementing a pass system, so that we can keep track of people's comings and goings.

"Splendid," Mayor Stern and James Coaltonstone said at the same time.

"Bill and Jethro used to work for Senator Puffy, Sir.

"Oh, isn't that the Senator who is accused of double dipping?" Mayor Stern enquired.

"Yes sir he is."

"Then I would guess that Jethro and Bill are very knowledgeable in the art of surveillance techniques." James Coaltonstone stated as he took a sip from the flask which he always concealed in his jacket pocket.

"Yes Sir. That is right; they are very knowledgeable and have connections to our Government's Official Directors surveillance equipment," John Bell confirmed.

"Are they for or against this Minese Exclusion League? Mine's Seven and eight have been hiring primarily Minese. The Minese are good workers, dependable, and they demand very little as long as we are willing and able to send their bones back to their home country after seven years from the day of their death. This is why Mine Seven and Mine Eight are economically feasible to run and Mine Five is not." James Coaltonstone said as he took another sip from his flask.

"The original meeting was mostly about designing a pass system so that we can determine who is illegal and who is authorized to be living in Coalton valley. Since the pit explosion we have considering the escalating of our pass system."

"And what about Deep Coal and his sharing of internal data with the PPZ," James Coaltonstone said as eyed the detectives up and down.

"The usual suspects are being watched very closely sir," John Bell said as he looked over his notes.

"Well they better be. That Ginger Goodwin is no fool. If it is him, it will not be easy to catch him in the act," James said as he exhaled cigar smoke.

"James, once we are under a state of emergency, we will have the authority to detain anyone as we see fit, regardless if we have evidence or not," Mayor Stern said as John Bell nodded.

"Sir if I may add, I think we should be careful that we don't provoke the crowd. The threat of being placed in glass cage is known to drive the weaker minds into psychosis." Don Bell said as he glanced at Susan Jones hoping that she would back him up.

"Sir, we need to rescue Ginger first before we can arrest him," Susan said nervously.

"Susan."

"I am sorry Mr. Stern."

"First we extract Goodwin from the pit, then we arrest him, then we find the evidence. I also suggest as the militia constructs our secondary security fence we should authorize the inclusion of Walmart, Wendy's and McDonalds within its perimeters," James Coaltonstone said in one breath and smoke escaped from his nostrils.

"Yes that is a splendid idea James," Ted Stern said admiringly. "That way the outsiders with campers can continue to camp at Walmart and eat at McDonalds and Wendy's."

"Do you think we should inform our stakeholders?" Susan asked.

"Certainly, but we will do it after we declare a state of emergency and after the walls are up," James Coaltonstone and Ted Stern said at the same time.

"Our cadets must still be paid over time but daily eight hour shifts are free to us, and the academy will be paying the cadets with credit earned toward their credentials," John Bell explained feeling exceptionally tired.

"I think it is mostly our local senator who is stirring up negative feelings against the Minese. Not all of them are here illegally." Mayor Stern said; not yet sure what side of the controversy he should be taking.

"That A.B. Peel and his Exclusion League cronies, will never get my vote. He is always stirring up local miners. All he wants is their vote; nothing more and nothing less," James Coaltonstone complained trying not to sound as agitated as he felt.

"My wife is on the Pitville Outreach Committee. She always welcomes those people. We don't believe in the 'not in our backyard' philosophy. That sort of snobbery does not come from us but it seems that the Exclusion League is growing legs." Mayor Stern said hoping to clarify his liberal standing in the community.

What will Jethro and Bill be doing?" James Coaltonstone enquired.

"Officially Jethro and Bill's duties will be secret," John Bell explained.

"They will be spying," Don said.

"Not exactly Don. We will be mixing with the riff-raff below there, and we are also looking into whether any of the illegals know about Mina's high altitude testing of nuclear testing. These tests in outer space," Bill explained.

"I thought those sort of tests were illegal now since the last few tests fried underground cables, telephone wires and street lights," Susan said while writing down notes.

"Yes, they are, and so is illegal mining. The Pitville Airbase depends on satellites and we believe it is not beyond the Minese capability to use high-altitude electromagnetic pulses, which is usually referred to EMPs, to kill our satellites. Nuclear weapons testing in space will also create a an artificial radiation belt which can kill our satellites too, even unintentionally.

"Why us? Why here? Why not stick to illegal mining and fuel their war machine that way?" Don Bell asked.

"Possibly because we have a base here, we also had what the Minese are interpreting as suspicious experimental explosions which some conspiracy theorists are attributing to the reason why Pitville and Buzzard Creek high schools were closed down due two hundred students in one school alone getting sick."

"We know why so many students fell ill so quickly," Ted Stern said. "Our students fell ill due to a regrettable outbreak of the Norwalk virus and nothing more. There is not one shred of evidence that the recent experimental explosions have anything to do with our students becoming ill so suddenly," Ted Stern said in defense of the local base.

"And we have no proof it wasn't. We don't even have proof that is it was the Norwalk virus any more than we have proof that the sudden illness was the direct result of the experimental explosions," Susan said as she avoided eye contact.

"Changing the topic slightly; I am deeply concerned that the Minese Exclusion League is gaining legs due to all these rumors being spread about. I think we need to stay focused on the pit fire and what we can do about it so it is controlled. I am very concerned that fires that seem to have no other explanation are occurring so randomly, and I have said it before, I believe that the explosion in Mine Five was caused by lightning. I need Mine Eight to be producing dividends for my shareholders from the Old Countries. We have invested millions into that mine, and as you know we are still building tunnels to connect our newly installed railway lines and harbor fronts. We are even building a tunnel under Coaltonstone Manor. We must not let the Minese Exclusion League ruin, my, our plans," James Coaltonstone said as he looked around to make sure that everyone was listening to him.

"I would like to discuss our plans concerning the out of town militia members and our need to card those outsiders surrounding our security fence and local riff-raff who may want to agitate this sensitive situation." John Bell, head of security said as he played with his wilting lettuce.

"Do you really think that is necessary to card all those people who came here to support Ginger? Don Bell asked still feeling guilty that his assistant in his department which was responsible for mine safety was trapped in Mine Five.

"Of course not! We just need to card the ones who look suspicious," John replied while glaring at his twin.

"Remember you two, wear your nametags. Last thing we need today is somebody getting you two mixed up. You John must be clearly identifiable as head of security as you Don must be clearly identifiable as head of mine safety," James Coaltonstone said while he watched Susan take notes.

"Susan why are you taking notes. What we are discussing is supposed to be secret."

"I am sorry sir.'

"It is okay Susan as long as you take those notes and shred them this instant. We don't need to be giving Deep Coal, whoever he may be, inside information and remember we all must tip toe lightly around that security fence. Remember there are more of them than us and the parents of those cadets vote. I don't want any of them getting hurt. I would like to place a motion that we raise the hotel tax.

"I will second that motion Ted," James said.

"I will third it," John Bell added.

"Why do we always meet in the board room at the Pitville Inn whenever we are going to raise taxes?" Susan asked.

"It is tradition," Mayor Stone replied.

"I must continue with my expansion," James Coaltonstone said as he took a drink from his flask. "John Bell, please stand up and report on our enforcement strategy."

Susan stood up and walked towards the window. Mayor Stern stood up and did the same thankful for the opportunity to change the subject.

"I have never seen a Minese in anyone's backyard. They keep to themselves as far as I know."

"Susan," Mayor Stern interjected before James Coaltonstone interrupted him.

"Most of the Minese have spent the best years of their lives here. They send money home to their families. They don't ask for much. They are so hard working. And their labor has built this region just as much as anyone's have. I think this Minese Exclusion League business is deplorable and despicable."

"This view is splendid. I can see the drones and the ship carrying our supplies from here," Susan said before she was interrupted.

"Susan, please," Mayor Stern interjected.

"Drones? Are those drones going to be used to spy on all those people waiting to meet Ginger?" Don Bell asked. Don still considered himself to be the head safety manager for Mine five until notified otherwise.

"I think those Drones are meant to be protecting our shipment."

"Shipment of what?

"John, control your brother or I will have to send him somewhere dark and gloomy to count things, it is hard enough to follow this conversation as it is," James Coaltonstone ordered.

"We are in the final stages of re-negotiating our lease, with the Government's Official Directors. The city has agreed to manage the operation of Buzzard Creek Dump for the next twenty five years," Mayor Stern said. "I really do think Ginger's concerns related to the fire hazard posed by our dump's present location are grandiose, to say the least.

"My guess is that Ginger is right sir. There is smoke coming out of the sidewalk, smoke coming out of the mountain area, it is just a matter of time smoke starts to come out of Buzzard Creek Dump," Susan Jones said before James Coaltonstone slammed his big fist down on the table in a fit of rage and yelled "What?"

"Now, Susan what did we say about talking. Your role is to take notes. As mayor, I am the one who assesses value placed on anyone, anything, and any place. Am I making myself clear, Susan?" Mayor Stern asked in a condescending tone which made Don soothe with anger as he typed on his com phone.

"I am glad to see someone is sitting quietly and taking notes; good work Don," James Coaltonstone said approvingly.

"Sir what is that glow coming out of that container ship?

"My god, that ship is on fire, I think we are under attack," Mayor Stern warned as he screamed and ducked under the table where he found James Coaltonstone already under and still smoking his cigar.

Chapter 4

December 25th 2030, around 7:00 p.m.

"Good evening to all and welcome back to 'Black Times' broadcasting live from the Pitville Hotel. As you can see behind me the entire fleet of Pitville ambulances are being employed to serve the injured, which may be at least a hundred. The container ship, King Coal, was carrying flammable goods from the mainland, when this terrible tragedy occurred. At this time we do not know officially what those goods were. Some reports are describing these goods to be explosives. This matter is under investigation and authorities are not speaking to any PPZ representative. Nevertheless we have a familiar face with us this evening, Doctor Smith.

"Thank you, Dr. Smith it very good of you to join us at such short notice."

"Well I can't stay long. I have many patients to attend. Glass was shattered all the way from Pitville Hotel where Mayor Stern was in a closed meeting and was covered in glass."

"Was Mayor Stern seriously injured? Are there others were injured? It seems there isn't a day that goes by where there isn't some horrible disaster occurring in Pitville," Dianne Black noted.

"It are sure getting our share of disasters. Windows exploded all along Main Street. The injured are filling the hospital emergency room, and I have never seen anything like this before. When the ship exploded it was not too far from Pitville Harbour which is right downtown, across from the street from the Pitville Hotel."

"How many people do you estimate have been hurt by shattered glass, Doctor Smith?"

"It is too early to know. So far there must be at least a hundred people, including Mayor Stern, who are being treated for glass related injuries.

Chapter 5

December 25th 2030, around 7:15 p.m.

Why is it whenever that Dianne Black talks to us I feel defensive and angry?" Jay wondered out loud.

"I don't know," Kevin replied.

"You are always on the defensive."

"No I am not, George."

"Okay!"

"I know what it is. I feel she keeps projecting these stereotypes onto us. She starts us at zero as if we didn't exist before she interviewed us. When the interview is over I think of all the things I wish she had asked me that are more important than the things that she actually did ask me," Jay said.

"I agree with Jay," Sam said. "And what really gets me upset is the way Ginger is being ignored while his lung condition is worsening by his entrapment."

"Exactly! And the entrapment keeps expanding as if we were all on different sides. Even getting this free alcohol instead of free energy drinks bugs me."

Chapter 6

December 25th 2030, around 8:00 p.m.

Are you sure that we are going the right way?" Kevin asked as he was feeling miserable and tired. The weight of the oxygen tank had taken its toll as he crawled behind his friends. The smell was horrid, and the smoke made seeing clearly very difficult.

"Of course I am sure," Sam said. This is our mine too. This is our coal and those illegals are stealing it from us. We go in there, and take their cable hoister and any equipment that we can get. If they chase us we show them our guns and then demand their lamps, then we get out and we close over the shaft opening the way we should have done a long time ago. We are getting Ginger out and we are going to give him a hero's welcome while he is still able to breathe."

"We can do it," Kevin said. "We just have to keep up the momentum."

"You mean act faster than the Minese. There they are," George said as loud as he could while whispering.

"Are you sure that we are going the right way? Why are there so many of them?" Same asked as his voice betrayed his fear and anxiety.

"I thought these tunnels would be more primitive than these," Jay said.

"What are all these crates for?" Sam asked no one in particular.

"I don't know. The signal is coming from over there and it is really strong," George said.

"I have never been on this side of Section E before; I never knew this section was so I have never seen such a nice looking pit railway before, I wonder where it goes." Jay said.

"What do you think is in all these crates? This tunnel sure doesn't smell anything like coal to me," Sam asked.

"You boys, stand up!" Ono commanded. He was a big Minese man holding onto his super-sized gun as tightly as he could; just in case his broken English was misunderstood. "What you do snooping around here?"

"We need help," George said.

"Help to do what? You look ignorant and sloppy." Ono said.

"Who are you to call us ignorant and sloppy?" Sam replied.

"We are all miners. We should respect that. I am George Smoothman, the morning crew's foreman. We need help freeing our friend and colleague, Ginger Goodwin. He freed us now we must free him. Only person on the surface who seems to be doing his best to organize a rescue is Ginger's grandfather, everyone else is sitting around, or building a wall around the security wall."

"We down here, including the ones who have passed to the other side, know who you speak of. The man who is now called deep coal by James Coaltonstone is on our side. Ginger Goodwin put his crew before himself. We go together and then go through tunnels and use gear that is in Mine Eight. I have key to door but this must remain secret. No one must ever know."

"What do you need?" Ono asked.

"We need at least a 1,200 foot ladder and air tanks," George said.

"I have a better idea. We get the tanks and back up batteries, and a stretcher, and we carry Ginger from the Safety Chamber and use the shaft lift to bring him out to the surface in Mine Eight," Ono suggested.

"If it is that easy why didn't control room arrange the same thing? Jay asked.'

"Mine Eight is not a coal mine. It is not official and no one would dare to question James Coaltonsmore, especially if he wins the election," Ono replied.

"You really think James Coaltonstone has a chance against A.B. Peel and his Exclusion League backers?" Jay asked.

"You don't?" Ono replied.

"So is Mine 8 just a coal mine then?" George asked.

"Of course not. Mine Eight is a Hemp Plantation. What you see, stays with you. We will get Ginger out, but we must never explain how. That will be the hard part."

"Is Mine Eight guarded?"

"No one guards what doesn't exist. If Mine Eight were guarded, someone would notice.

Chapter 7

December 25th 2030, around 9:00 p.m.

"And why wasn't the ventilation shaft in Section E made wide enough so that it could be used as an escape shaft?" Lance Diamond asked James Coaltonstone?

"We never thought an emergency exit would be necessary. Anyway having a second escape exit wasn't required, so did our best to keep expenses down so that we could stretch the limited resources that we had," James Coaltonstone replied defensively.

"Hold on, that young doctor, Dr. Ashley Knight just sent me an email." Lance said as he turned around and opened it. James stood on his toes to look over his shoulder.

"Is it about the baby?" James asked.

"I don't know, let me read it. James, this is private."

"Email isn't that private."

'Well this one is. It is addressed to me because it is private correspondence with a physician. James. Please will you give me some privacy?

"It is very long. It seems to be about some tests that my personal physician ordered last month, back home. Oh these doctors, they never tell you what you want to hear. She is advising rest. My God, I am the only one doing anything around here. If I could I would snap my fingers and just make everyone do their job. Instead, everyone is sitting around waiting for a member from G.O.D. to tell them what to do. I must free my grandson from that hell hole that you run, and I cannot do that while resting. Just look around. Everyone is resting. No one is doing anything but resting. My grandson is 1,200 feet below the surface without a basic escape route. As Ginger's lung condition worsens, as we speak, this doctor is telling me to rest?

"Are you ill?"

"Of course not."

"Ginger will be dead soon, if we don't get him out of that hell hole."

"Let me read that letter."

"No, you can't. I deleted it."

Chapter 8

December 25th 2030, around 9:30 p.m.

"To all my faithful viewers welcome back to 'Black Times. All of us at the PPZ wish that Mayor Stern has a speedy recovery. The container ship 'King Coal' exploded just minutes before it was to dock at Pitville Harbor. There were at least a hundred people lining up in the Pitville's Emergency Rooms, needing treatment from shattered glass. More on this news breaking story as it unfolds," Dianne paused for a moment and then began reading the next page of her script.

"It is hard to believe that it has been only two days since the early morning explosion in Mine Five, which occurred 1,200 feet below Pitville, a small town situated in the beautiful Coalton Valley," Dianne Black explained as she spoke into the microphone."

"While we speak, we are walking towards the Miners' Cafeteria. There is George A. Smoothman, foreman for the morning crew sitting at the head of that table in the center of the Miner's Cafeteria. Good evening Mr. Smoothman. Do you have a few words to share with the world?"

"Good evening, Dianne, thank you for having me on your show. As the head foreman of the morning crew, I witnessed how Ginger Goodwin prevented us from walking into a pending mine Explosion early Sunday Morning by putting our safety before his own. If it wasn't for Ginger Goodwin we would all be trapped in Mine Fine or worse, instead of just him."

"Thank you, Mr. Smoothman."

"And sitting beside Mr. Smoothman is Jay T. Paylor, Assistant Foreman of the morning crew."

"Good evening Mr. Paylor, would you like to share a word with our faithful 'Pitville Mine Disaster' viewers this evening?"

"I sure do. I would like to wish everyone a Merry Christmas. As the assistant foreman, I am second in command; therefore I will delegate myself to cutting the second piece of cake and to opening the second bottle of beer even though this is actually my first. As you can see, here we are having Ginger Goodwin's birthday party and our own Christmas party all in one. We would also like to report that Ginger was wearing his birthday hat, but we can't. Here is to you Bro. I would like to wish a speedy recovery to Mayor Stern and to all of those injured in the container ship explosion, which happened just a little while ago,"

"Thank you, Mr. Paylor."

"Hold on, I am not done. If it wasn't for Ginger Goodwin, we would have been trapped down in that pit, instead of him. Ginger left the safety of his office and actually descended into the mine before we did. He was investigating why the gas monitor numbers were not being transmitted."

"Do you know why these numbers were not being transmitted, Mr. Paylor?"

"Yes, I do, because the methane monitor had been turned off by someone."

"How do you know that, Mr. Paylor?"

"Ginger sent a message to Christina, Ginger's fiancée, right after he realized that someone had turned the monitor off. I really hope that this matter gets investigated as soon as possible, and I really hope that Ginger Goodwin is rescued before something horrible happens to him. I hate to say this but I am starting to believe in the Black Diamond Curse."

"Come on Jay," George scolded.

"Thank you Mr. Smoothman and Mr. Paylor. I am Dianne Black bringing to you live coverage from the heart of the Pitville mine disaster of 2030."

"Hold on we are not done. We want to say that we don't know much about the Pitville Harbor explosion. We have been in the Miners' Cafeteria all day, which is in the basement and doesn't have any windows and the news we are given is regulated. We want to make sure that the focus stays on rescuing Ginger. We are concerned that rescuers from out of town may rely too much on the maps they are given. Many of the tunnels down below have never been mapped or documented."

"I am sorry Mr. Paylor, we are pressed for time. We need to get to the hospital and interview some of the victims of the container explosion and of course we must hear from our sponsors. I am sure that the professionals are thankful for your concern, but they know more about what is going on down there than you do."

"Right! I have only been working down there for fifteen years, so what do I know?" Jay replied sounding hurt.

"And another issue which is being ignored is all this rain. You didn't ask us what we thought about all this rain and how it could hamper rescuing Ginger while making the conditions in the mine worse and more acidic."

"You must know by now, Mr. Paylor, I am not PPZ's weather girl. I understand your concern, but this story is about the mine disaster."

"This rain could make the flooding in Mine Five more dangerous for Ginger."

"I am sorry Mr. Paylor, Dianne said before Jay grabbed the mike from Dianne.

"Hold on. I want to know something. When are they getting Ginger out of the pit?"

"You have to be patient. I heard that Coaltonstone Mines is providing you with all these refreshments free of charge. James Coaltonstone is doing his best."

"If that disaster down in the pit had been prevented we could have been celebrating with Ginger. And we would have had enough money of our own to pay for our own party," Jay said forgetting to hide the hostility he was feeling.

"I am sure that you are very tired, Mr. Paylor. The Government's Official Directors will do everything they can to assist all of Coaltonstone mines' employees."

"Did G.O.D. actually say that?" And what is James Coaltonstone actually doing to help us miners recover from our pay loss?

"As far as I know James Coaltonstone will be arranging loans for you all. Goodbye and Merry Christmas."

"And now a word from our sponsor," Steve Jones said as he watched the interaction from his PPZ control room at the Eagle Eye Inn.

Chapter 9

December 25th 2030, around 10:00 p.m.

"You know I feel like we are wasting our lives here," Kevin said as he sipped on his third beer.

"Aww, you just feel that way because we almost lost our lives today and everyone else is going about as if we are not in the loop anymore. Don't forget that thousands of people are congregating around the Admin building and Mine Five, waiting for Ginger to show his red head. It not like we are really alone," George said as he faced Jay.

Jay replied, "Sure we are being forgotten. Now we are out of work we are nothing. We have no function. And this loan business that James Coaltonstone is pushing on us doesn't just scare me, it makes me angry. We don't need more debt and James Coaltonstone doesn't need more money."

"We are all feeling out of the loop. Wanting a way in and a way out," George said looking at Sam Jones for support."

"Who doesn't wish for a way out of Pitville?" Sam said.

"And where would we go?" Kevin asked his cousin.

"Talk about needing a way out. Just think about Ginger. He really needs a way to escape his situation. If we start feeling defeated now how is Ginger supposed to feel tomorrow and the next day? Ginger hasn't lost the battle yet and we need to be there encouraging him to remain strong and positive until we get him out of there," Jay said.

"We sure look like we have lost the battle. We have lost our bonuses; we have lost our jobs which means we have lost the entitlement to company owned homes. Ginger is still stuck down there in the pit with no one is doing anything except saying sweet nothings," Kevin replied.

"Well Ginger's grandfather is giving the Coaltonstones a run for their money," Sam said. "So changing the subject a bit; I wonder how much free beer the Coaltonstones will give us before we become pitiful alcoholics," Sam said.

"It seems that everything around here is done around us, to us, and against us. Instead of someone in the know telling us what is really going on, they leave us out of the loop, they start us at zero whenever they speak to us so we never get ahead, and whatever we say makes us appear as if we don't know what is going on," Kevin said.

"Well we don't," Sam replied.

"Yeah, I know what Kevin and Sam are saying. It is not just our lives being turned upside down that makes us angry. You have all seen my mother sitting outside rain or shine waiting for the mail ever since the Harris family's mailbox was stolen. Well, two days ago, a man came around with some contraption to measure distance, and he was measuring the property lines surrounding my mother's house. My mother said that the only thing the man said to her was you better get out of the way if you don't want your picture taken. And then he took about five pictures of her house and left, leaving my mother worried cause she had no idea what was going on. It could have been the city, it could have been the bank, it could have been someone mapping buildings on top of undocumented coal deposits though her house was the only one she noticed was having its property line measured," Sam wasn't sure what to say next so he took a sip of his beer.

"If Ginger were here you know what he would say," Kevin said while he ate two peanuts.

"Yes, he would say that we are at the bottom of this crony capitalism which only favors those in the loop and locks everyone else out.

"Yes, and if anyone hears us talking like this, we could be accused of being communists, so tone it down," Sam whispered nervously.

"Hey guys George just got a skype message from Christina," Jay said as took a closer look at the tiny print.

"Stop looking over my shoulder Jay, this could be private which means a confidential message," George responded trying to sound like he was still in charge. "I know it says confidential, but it isn't private the way some messages are and maybe we share what Christina is seeing up there. So I will read it out loud," George added.

Confidential:

Skype message to George Smoothman (Foreman of the Morning Crew) from Christina Watson (Accounting Assistant to Alex Coaltonstone).

Hi George:

I don't know what to say first. The visit with Ginger was far too short. I returned to my office, even though I could have just gone home, in theory anyway, I am being told I have to stay here. While everyone is celebrating I feel so awful that Ginger isn't rescued yet.

You won't believe this, but they are building the wall higher. Of all the things they could be doing right now, they are spending money on building a wall. The cadets and the militia are working on the wall together as if the crowd weren't standing there watching.

There are lots of new people congregating. I can see them through my window. They have the whole area lit up. The public is as close to the admin building and mine as they will be allowed to be.

The timing is so bad I think the wall is being built for no other purpose than to antagonize the public to act out a self-fulfilling prophecy. That is what it feels like anyway, George. I just sit here, watching and waiting.

The crowd of people around the security fence is growing. I can't imagine how many people there must be now. Tens of thousands I suppose.

I wish there were more rescue workers, and more machinery and drills coming in. Nothing seems to be happening. Ginger's grandfather is vowing that if one way doesn't work then another way will have to be found.

James Coaltonstone and Mayor Stern seem to be ok after the explosion at the hotel. They have small band aids stuck here and there and are mingling with the crowd passing out pizza vouchers; which seems very strange since they are probably the ones in charge of the admin relating to building the wall.

They are also passing around boxes of pizza as shifts begin and end for the cadets behind the security fence. So I hope you guys are having a bit of fun at the party. I suppose you can't really see what is going on like I can. Remember Dr. Knight told us all to stay positive.

Yours Friend Forever Christina Watson (almost Christina Goodwin)

"What do you think we should do, Jay?" Kevin asked.

"Don't know. Those illegals must have all the equipment that we need? They work against us just like everyone else does. If we have to ask permission to do something why don't they? We follow the rules and look at us now; we are jobless. The illegals are still working so they must have all kinds of equipment. I say we get into Mine 2 and descent into mine six and then tunnel into section E of Mine Five. That way we can use what is available and avoid the area that unstable in Mine Five," Jay said.

"Well if it is that simple why isn't G.O.D.'s rescue team down there already?" Kevin asked.

"Because it won't be simple. Rescues are never simple or even safe," George said.

"So what? Nothing we do is safe," Jay replied.

"How are supposed to do something when we are being cut off as we speak from the other side of the wall. We still have our passes, so we probably could get back in again. Ginger is more important anyway." Sam said.

"We could use those old tunnels that link Mine Five to Mine Eight. Once we get what we need maybe we could try. I mean those tunnels are also being used as the ventilation system for the illegals or that is what I hear anyway." Kevin said.

"It sounds dangerous." Sam said a little louder than he meant to. "My wife wants me to quit mining. She keeps telling me how much she loves me, which is a good thing, but then she adds that I am on borrowed time."

"I agree with Kev. We go into their neck of the woods, where the illegals mine, we grab all their cables and oxygen tanks and throw some fire crackers at them before we leave. That is the only way that we can get Ginger out of that hell-hole in a timely fashion. Everything and everyone, who isn't with us with us on this, is against us. We have no reason to wait or care about anyone who is not with us on this. We need to take this situation into our own hands, for Ginger's sake." Jay said.

"If we take the illegals' headlamps and leave them in the dark they will be helpless," Sam noted.

"Exactly, then we can seal them in," Jay replied. "No one will know what happened. Everything and everyone is working against us and no one cared much that we almost died."

"All they give us is poison," Sam said.

"Agreed; the more we drink the more we play into the stereotypes they create about us. Life is hard for all of us. Nowadays without money we are nothing. And even with money we are glared at by those who consider that they are on the upper rung of the ladder. This is what divides us all the time."

"You mean our races?" Sam asked

"No, of course not, I mean our position on the ladder divides us. And we all want to be on a higher rung. And someone who seems to be on a higher rung is always looking over their shoulder at us and you know the look," George replied.

"Yeah, that look," Sam said.

"That accusatory, suspicious, you must be Jack the Ripper look that fills you with fatalistic doubt about yourself and your future," Kevin said.

"Every time someone gives me that look I feel they are only seconds away from pushing their panic button and I will be taken away to a hard-labor camp in the Arctic never to be allowed to climb the ladder again," Sam said.

"Yes, pushed off the ladder for evermore." George said

"The Minese miners are closer to us in rank than we are to James Coaltonstone," George said.

"That is for sure," Sam said.

"Coaltonstone gave us this beer. We should be thankful for something. He hasn't given us anything else yet. I bet he is going to make us beg," Jay said.

"Or at least borrow. I don't like the idea of fighting with the Minese. They are miners just like we are," George Smoothman said.

"No, they are not like us. They are on this Island illegally. They take our jobs," Jay said.

"Are you sure they are not like us? Someone brings them here and they seem to be doing work that would be too unsafe and illegal for us to do, since we are quasi protected by safety regulations," George said.

"Right; we could have all been trapped in the mine explosion on Sunday. And Ginger is just waiting, hoping to be rescued. What else can he do? This is his fourth day down there. You are sounding like Ginger, and look where it got him. When it comes to money, greed takes over. **One side wins and one side loses.** Of course it is war," Jay said.

"Well, sort of. Everything, now, seems to be engineered to be like war. We are all fighting to climb to the next rung of the ladder. The ladder is like the common ground; so people are led to believe that it benefits them to provoke each other into a feud which leads to the one on the lower rung into trouble, then pushed down the ladder. We all see the games being played even in Pitville Grocery. We are stared at as if we are going steal something. We have these negative projections thrown at us when spoken to. If we respond, we appear just like the stereotypes they are projecting onto us, sometimes trapping us in their sum-zero role play. They turn around and stare at us as if we are following them when we walk in in the door. Sometimes the door is let to swing in our face." George said.

"Tell me about it," Sam said

"They check our bags for drugs, knives and weapons as if we actually have those things. And they do it over and over again, until we feel that it is normal for them to treat us this way. If we ask a clerk where something is, they sometimes tell us, and sometimes they don't. Sometimes we say something to them they accuse us of swearing at them and then threaten to ban us from the only grocery store in town. That is manufactured exclusion if I have ever felt it. Then we have no job even our wives may stop speaking to us. If the bots take more of our management jobs, there will be fewer rungs on the ladder to climb, and then there will be more reason to be at each other's throats. If we get treated as if we are the scum of the Earth for too long we start believing that we are. And they treat us like that, so they can feud with us, and push us to an even lower rung of the collective ladder," George said.

"Ginger tried to reason with them. And look where he is now. We do what we are told and now most of us have some form of lung disease and are broke and are treated like the scum of the Earth. And if we are not careful, we start believing that we are. Nothing works in our favor and time is shorter for us than those who were lucky enough to find work up on the surface," Kevin said.

"We can't let the 'doggie eat doggie' culture poison our state of mind. We must see what could have been the way Ginger does." George said.

"Ginger is a visionary because he has the courage to be a visionary; that is why we have to get him out of there. He is one of a kind." Jay said.

"To win, we must think like winners, the way James Coaltonstone does. To find a better way we must see the state of things as visionaries, the way Ginger does." George said.

"You know why nothing works for us?" Jay said.

"Why?" Sam asked.

"We don't make the decisions. People with money and power make the decisions and those decisions turn our lives upside down. I remember how Mathew kept saying, before he was crushed on July 4th, 2021; that one day, one of was going to get crushed by that old continuous mining machine while that horrible boss bot whistles and yells at us," Jay replied.

"And Mathew always prayed that it wouldn't be him," Kevin added.

"I remember Mathew actually kneeling praying," Sam said.

"And in the end it was him that was crushed. Now Christina is getting pushed around by Bots R Us just the way we all get pushed around," Jay said.

"It is not that I don't agree with you all, I do agree with you all, but I think we should wait until we sober up," George said wisely.

"When we sober up we won't be as brave. Did you see Ginger coughing on the com-screen, I don't think he is going to last much longer if he doesn't get out of there soon," Kevin said.

"I agree with Kevin," Jay said.

"Ok, assume that I am in; how are we supposed to get Ginger out of there any faster than those heavy duty outfits waiting for the okay to go in?" George asked.

"Because we are going to try, and all they are doing is waiting for someone from G.O.D. to tell them to go in. Ginger needs us. It is a crime to let a man die on his birthday," Jay said.

"Totally agreeable with Jay," Kevin replied. "All we have to do is take the equipment from the illegals. If they can get into the shafts with their harnesses and cables and battery operated generators, we can too."

"We are healthier and smarter so we have the advantage," Jay said.

Sam started to cough uncontrollably again. He took his green puffer out of his pocket and inhaled his medication.

"We are also bigger than most of the Minese, in many ways tunneling is a lot easier for them," George said.

"So you think the Minese will just hand us their equipment?" Sam asked.

"Of course not. We will have to use force to take it from them," Jay replied.

"How many Minese are there down there?" Sam asked.

"Don't know. We should take this beer with us," Jay replied.

Chapter 10

December 25th 2030, around 11:00 p.m.

Welcome viewers to Black Times. I am Dianne Black on location to report yet another disaster in Pitville. This time the victim is no other than Pitville's very own James Coaltonstone, owner and the Chief Executive Officer of Coaltonstone Mines and associate of the Big Seven Coal Group .

"Welcome to our show Mr. Coaltonstone."

"Thank you Dianne, under other circumstances it would be a pleasure to be here.

"Could you please tell our loyal viewer what actually happened?"

"Well I am not actually sure what happened. I was taking my private train to my home. As you know I have a private train station nearby our administrative building which connects to our mines. It was a terrible feeling when the earth sank beneath my tracks."

"I bet. Mr. Coaltonstone, can you tell our audience how such a terrifying event could happen to the CEO of Coaltonstone Mines.

"There has been a terrible problem in Pitville. We have thieves who routinely steal our Anthracite Coal Pillars since they are so valuable. These pillars are holding mines and part of my railway together. When they are stolen there is often a danger of infrastructure collapsing. My guess is that some evil person, probably an illegal, stole my coal pillars which were holding up my railway track infrastructure. It is lucky no one was hurt. These coal pillar thefts are getting out of hand. One day someone is going to get killed."

"Why do you think there are so many disasters plaguing Pitville and your mining operation? Do you think there is some truth that these events are due to the curse of the Black Diamond or is it just an accumulation of bad management practices over the years?"

"What kind of question is that? Dianne; when a pillar is stolen under a private railway, my conclusion can only be that our society is in terrible decline. I am ordering 24 hour guard duty, effective immediately, to protect what is left of my assets."

"And what will your security team do if they catch the person who is allegedly stealing the pillars."

"Shoot him if necessary. What do you mean alleged? It is obvious the pillars that were under my Railway are missing. I will not allow those illegals to ruin me or endanger the safety of my crew and family. Endangering my private railway is the last straw. And I hope you riff-raff are listening out there, because I am speaking to you."

"Now that we have you in real life, can you tell our viewers when Ginger Goodwin's rescue will begin?

"For security concerns, our current plans cannot be shared with the public at this time. Dianne, if I may, I would like to make a very important announcement. I am seeking nomination to run for president in the coming election so that I can give that A.B. Peel and his Exclusion League cronies a run for their money. And one of my promises will be to expose Deep Coal, whoever he may be, for I am sure he is behind this pillar theft and possibly even the explosion which occurred at Pitville harbor on Christmas day as well as Sunday's early morning Pit Five explosion. Those illegals and their cohorts must be stopped or our way of life will be ruined forever."

"Can you summarize the steps which need to be engineered before rescuing Ginger Goodwin from Mine Five can begin?

"Not really. We are trying our best, which is all that I can promise. Good Day, Dianne."

"Mr. Coaltonstone before you leave, you must tell us whether the rumors are true. Are you Ginger Goodwin's biological father?"

"Preposterous. Mr. Goodwin is my primary suspect in the Deep Coal data theft and I am also wondering if he is involved in this pillar being stolen under my railway. Did you know that Mr. Goodwin calls me a crony capitalist behind my back? I know this because I have heard it with my own ears while he was socializing with that George Smoothman and Jay Paylor. No son of mine would betray me in such a way."

"Are you saying that Lance Diamond is lying and did you just say that you have the Miners' Cafeteria under surveillance?

"You can't possibly believe that I am going to answer such loaded questions? This interview is now over."

Thank you, Mr. Coaltonstone.

"One more thing; as president of Tut Island I will be personally involved in establishing railways to connect the world starting with a railway to connect Eurasia with North America by building a bridge across the Bering Strait. I believe that the railway could connect the whole planet and help bridge the gap between the have nations and the have not nations. As president of Tut Island I will make sure that our nonviolent prisoners are put to work putting out fires, especially the troublesome fire which is threatening Stonely Mountain and when they aren't putting out of fires they will be helping our cadets build our security wall.

"Thank you again for your time Mr. Coaltonstone."

"Hold on Dianne, I would like to announce that if I am elected as president of Tut Island I will not only legalize the hemp industry I will support, facilitate and revitalize the manufacturing sectors of Tut Island. We have external forces which threaten to disrupt our hailing economy, but I will make Tut Island great again."

"I thought tut Island was already great."

"Yes, but not the way it used to be, before the explosion in Mine Five, before Deep Coal betrayed the entire network of Coaltonstone Mines. And I promise you this if Mina continues to engage in High Altitude Nuclear Explosions which we know for a fact are able to turn off our street lamps, then we will hold back payments on our debt to that country. We must all agree to not test nuclear weapons in outer space. This practice is far too dangerous."

"Thank you again, Mr. Coaltonstone. Now, let us hear a word from our sponsor."

Chapter 11

December 26th 2030, around 8:00 a.m.

NEWS FLASH

The membership of G.O.D., the Tut Island chapter, have declared war on the Minese. Every able bodied man must sign up for service.

Chapter 12

December 26th 2030, around 9:00 a.m.

"Why are we having another back room meeting in my office?" Mayor Stern asked James Coaltonstone.

"Because I called another meeting because we need another meeting. We have to figure out why it is taking so long getting Mine Five back in operation," James Coaltonstone replied.

"I thought the drilling crews would have started their work by now." Mayor Stern said.

"Well they haven't. I owe the Minese and our own authorities tons of money. I am supposed to transform this coal into money, but I can't as long as the mine is closed.

"Well we have to wait until conditions are safe. There are a lot of union people working on this rescue operation and certain safety requirements have to be met," Mayor Ted Stern explained as if he were talking to a small child.

"I pay for results," James Coaltonstone said. "Otherwise I would go broke."

"Times are changing James," Mayor Stern said, almost whispering.

"I know exactly what you mean. Being able to do things fast and independently made me who I am today. I am the one taking the risk. It is my money tied up in that mine."

Ted Stern had never seen James Coaltonstone look so worried and defeated before and it scared him.

"Thank you for joining me this evening." Mayor Stern said as he observed the men who had joined him in his conference

49

room, in the south wing, of Pitville's City Hall. Don and John Bell's glum looks appeared to be contagious for. James Coaltonstone was not looking any happier.

"And thank you Susan for bringing us these refreshments so efficiently. Remember it is still Christmas Day," Mayor Stern said while trying to force a smile

"I thought the drilling crews would be more organized today," James Coaltonstone said before he helped himself to a piece of pizza and a bottle of beer. "I suppose on top of everything else, we are still under a water boil advisory?" James Coaltonstone grumbled as he removed the bottle cap with his teeth.

"That is right James. We just have to go with the flow and roll with the punches," Ted Stern replied a little too cheerfully.

"The mood outside is quite festive, Sir. It could have been a lot worse," Don Bell said.

"There are people clinging to the security fence. Others are decorating it with flowers," John Bell said. "I find this behavior very inappropriate," he added.

Chapter 13

December 26th 2030, around 10:00 a.m.

"Your honor, may I be allowed to use George A. Smoothman's journal and email to summarize the events which occurred early morning on the day of the explosion. Mr. Smoothman is foreman of the morning crew that Mathew Watson was working on. I am asking for this consideration, your honor because Mr. Smoothman is still missing," David Bell, joint council for Boss Bots R Us and Coaltonstone Mines proposed.

"I object," Jack Jones, council for the People said abruptly.

"Overruled; you may use Mr. Smoothman's journal, Mr. Bell," Judge Bell replied.

"Thank you, your honor."

You May proceed Mr. Jones.

"Ginger Goodwin, who is also missing, refused to certify that the mine was safe, on December 22nd, 2030, only moments before the explosion. I have asked for Mr. Goodwin's journal to use as evidence, but have been denied this request because it has been classified as Secret. I am asking once again if I could have access to Mr. Goodwin's journal."

"Permission denied," Judge Bell said.

"Sir, with all respect, Mr. Goodwin's professional opinion, as assistant safety manager, the mine's environmental conditions did not meet the accepted standard for mine safety.

I have a file, full of frantic skype messages praising Ginger's quick thinking which prevented the morning crew from descending into Mine Five at the regular starting time, but doing so left him trapped in the Mine. Due to his own quick thinking he managed to find his way to the safety chamber in Section E, where four on his crew, George Smoothman, Jay Paylor, Sam and Kevin Jones found a way to rescue him, but now all five of them are missing. So none of the men who were working in Mine Five at the time when Mathew Watson was crushed, back in 2021, are available to testify. So again, I request an adjournment until these men are found.

"Denied," Judge Bell retorted. "Just summarize Mr. Jones."

"Certainly, thank you, sir. On the morning of December 22nd, 2030, Ginger Goodwin showed his true colors. He would not allow the crew to descend into Mine Five until his safety inspection was complete. According to the witnesses who are not present at this time, the Whistle-Boss Bot 5C was whistling while hovering around Ginger Goodwin's head for at least twenty minutes. This is the same behavior that Whistle-Boss Bot 5C was acting out only seconds before Mathew Watson's accident, which occurred on July 4th, 2021. Whistle-Boss bots always whistle nonstop whenever there is a conflict of commands between the mine's safety department and the mine's productivity department are also in conflict. Both Mathew and Ginger had little control over the whistle-boss bot's whistling when their lives were put in danger. Often the whistling stops only after the boss bot files a complaint, which permanently degrades Coaltonstone Mines' employees' work record. For workers at this company, it is like being marked by the mechanical beast for life."

James Coaltonstone nudged his lawyer expecting to cue him to object to the submission of documents which did not flatter his operations and implied that Coaltonstone Mines had conspired to avoid legal and environmental safety standards in the pursuit of profit.

"Objection," David Bell said.

"Overruled," Judge Bell replied.

"Sir, this last statement by Mr. Jones is an opinion, not a fact and is inflammatory."

"I have noted your objection. Your objection is overruled because the atmosphere in the mine affects safety all the time."

"Mr. Jones continue and please refrain from the theatrics and drama."

"Thank you sir, I will sir. The people of Coalton Valley are regulated by these whistle-boss bots day and night. The whistle-boss bot whistles once at the end of each shift and whistles twice when the next shift begins. When there is an emergency the whistle-boss bot will whistle four times, if it is able to. If the whistle-boss bot is disabled, then the siren-bot, which belongs to the volunteer fire department, will kick in and do the whistle-bot's job, but only louder."

The audience in the court room couldn't help but laugh.

"Order in the court," Judge Bell demanded. "Please continue Mr. Jones."

"Alex Coaltonstone, Christina Watson's boss, and lead accountant for Mine Five, was very much old man James Coaltonstone's son. Alex Coaltonstone had scheduled recovery related tasks for Christina to do before the financial markets opened Monday morning, December 23rd, the day after the explosion in Mine Five. Christina was instructed to phone suppliers and the bank that day and asked for a ninety-day extension on all accounts payable. Christian Watson was also authorized to buy back COALT stock before the stock price fell the next day.

Don Bell is Ginger Goodwin's boss and lead administrator in Mine Five's Safety Department.

Don Bell's twin brother, John Bell, who is head of mine security, spends most of his time with John working out security issues related to operating Coaltonstone Mines. The day of the disaster, and December 22nd was no different

Mine Five has always under staffed so I find it hard to blame any one individual for this horrible nightmare. Well that is not entirely true. I do blame James Coaltonstone. He seems to have no scruples when cutting back expenses so he can increase his profits for himself and his cronies.

Alex Coaltonstone appeared to more concerned about the fate of Whistle-Boss Bot 5C and the chance that panic selling of COALT stock might spiral out of control tomorrow morning. Alex didn't even mention Ginger, he just told Christina to buy blocks of COALT stock as soon as analysts recommended selling. Sunday the financial market was closed, so panic selling of COALT stock could start as soon as world markets opened Monday morning. Anthracite coal is in high demand so it was possible that any event which threatened supply may drive the price of COALT stock up instead of down.

Christina asked Alex Coaltonstone if anyone was going to issue a press release related to rescuing Ginger Goodwin and salvage plans. Alex replied that he did not know. Christina Watson was shocked and thought that it would be prudent to have some form of communication with the public as soon as possible."

"Objection; Mr. Jones is mixing fact with hearsay."

"I will overrule this objection, but Please Mr. Jones, try to be less colorful."

The audience started to laugh again while Judge Bell demanded silence.

"Please continue Mr. Jones."

"Thank you, sir. Your honor, many of the issues which I am describing are in the missing miners' journals which have been assigned classified status and cannot be disclosed at this time without your permission, therefore I request again, that this case either be remanded until the missing miners are found or allow me to use Mr. Goodwin's journal," Jack Jones requested."

"Request denied. Court is adjourned. I will return to my chambers and once I have determined fault in this case you will all be notified. Good day."

Chapter 14
Email message to Muni Bugden: Confidential

December 26, 2030
Dear Christina:

I wanted to let you know from me. Your case has been decided in favor of Bots R Us. Judge Bell ruled that this case has been going on for way too long, according to the judge; our request to postpone the hearing day appeared to only serve to anger the judge. I am so sorry I can't represent you. This case has taken every penny that I have and I can't finance our Pro Bono arrangement any further. I am so sorry Christina.

With kind regards,
Muni Bugden (Attorney at Law).

****

Email message to Jay T. Paylor (Assistant Foreman for the morning crew)
Confidential

December 26, 2030:
Hi Jay:

Where are you? I saw Chief Cuff drive by in her ghost car. I always know it is her. She has that bumper sticker on her car advertising their 25K reward for reporting gang members. I really wish that I could report the Power Clique as a gang of conspirators. COALT stock is being sold off in huge blocks. This started Friday, about fifteen minutes before the market closed. Someone seems to have chosen the last day and the last fifteen minutes of so called open market, before Sunday's first explosion. Something is up. We are supposed to be sitting here quietly, while Ginger is down there breathing toxic fumes, someone is buying stock dirt cheap and all I hear is bullshit and stall tactics. Talk about gang bullying, disregarding the legislation which is supposed to keep ordinary people safe.

     I lost my case Jay. I am going to be a prisoner forced into involuntary servitude, spending imprisoned in a glass cage with no privacy for the rest of my life. I don't know what to do Jay. Where are you? Where is George? You were missed in court.

     Your friend forever, Christina Watson,

     (Accounting Assistant to Alex Coaltonstone).

Chapter 15
December 26th 2030, around 1:00 p.m.

In a closed meeting, Judge Bell ruled that the robot manufacturer Bots R Us was not negligent in the design of Boss bots. He also ruled that James Coaltonstone was not negligent. Judge Bell ruled that Bobby Coaltonstone was criminally negligent. After hours of expert opinions and testimony, the judge ruled that there was plenty of evidence showing criminal negligence during the design of the ventilation system and while monitoring coal dust. It was ruled that the gas explosion in Mine Five on December 22nd was Bobby Coaltonstone's fault and James Coaltonstone only benefitted from Bobby's recklessness because he owned the mine, not because he ordered Bobby to be reckless. The judge rules that Bobby had been reckless on his own. Coaltonstone Mines agreed to pay Ginger Goodwin an undisclosed amount for pain and suffering, but James is suing Ginger for intellectual property theft since he still believes that Ginger is Deep Coal.

An email written by an employee and wife Christina Watson of the deceased miner, Mathew Watson, was proof that much of the suffering endured while working in Mine Five at Coaltonstone Mines was preventable.

Chapter 16

December 26th 2030, around 2:00 p.m.

"I have a memo here that Doctor Knight is requesting more information related to the way we are softening the City's water supply. She suspects, that what used to be considered food related obesity is actually water retention to the process which creates added salt to our water. Have you ever heard of anything so radicicolous?" Mayor Stern was not expecting an answer.

"Sooner or later water will be the new gold," Susan Jones said.

"Now Susan what did I say about talking?" Mayor Stern said as he frowned.

"Without water nothing lives and everything turns brown and dies," Susan added.

"We will either have to find more water or dig up more coal, so that we can generate electricity for the next generation," John Bell said.

"Pitville was never designed to be anything more than a temporary mining town," James Coaltonstone remarked.

"Pity," Ted Stern added.

"I suppose no one will notice if Pitville grows darker and smellier and the ash-piles in Buzzard Creek just grow higher," Susan Jones said.

"Now Susan, what did I say about talking?" Mayor Stern scolded Susan on more time.

Chapter 17
December 26ᵗʰ 2030, around 3:00 p.m.

"Good afternoon viewers. I am Dianne Black and welcome to the Black Times show. I am bringing to you another live update from the Pitville Mine Disaster of 2030." Dianne announced as she tried to conceal her disappointment with the verdict.

"Judge Bell has ruled that even though there was a failure to monitor the buildup of gas minutes before the 5:20 AM explosion which occurred December 22ⁿᵈ, in Mine Five owned by Coaltonstone Mines, member of the Big Seven Coal group.

Judge Bell ruled that it could not be proven beyond the benefit of reasonable doubt that the monitor on the shearing machine had been turned off intentionally, therefore Judge Bell ruled that the cause of the explosion was accidental.

Judge Bell did rule against Bobby Coaltonstone, son of James Coaltonstone, CEO of Coaltonstone Mines. Judge Bell ruled that Mr. Bobby Coaltonstone was criminally negligent when operating as lead Ventilation Engineer. Judge Bell has ruled that Bobby Coaltonstone had taken risks with miners' safety to save money. Therefore he was the only one that has been found criminally negligent and has been sentenced to twenty six years of hard labor in the Arctic Mines.

The judge also ruled that it was reasonable to conclude that over the years Mine Five had been operating in a reckless fashion and was partially responsible for the death of Mathew Watson. A settlement between Mr. Watson's estate and Coaltonstone Mines had been agreed upon during the year of Mr. Watson's accident, 2021.

The judge also ruled that during the current war effort, Tut Island's alleys must rely on the region for it coal therefore the mine cannot be closed down, but will be watched very closely.

Alleged illnesses related to breathing coal dust will be addressed at a later date since their testimony is not relevant to the case at hand.

Judge Bell also ruled in favor of Bots R Us, leaving poor Christina Watson to pay, whatever way she can, ten years of legal costs."

"Without us today is Christina Watson, Welcome back to our show."

"Thank you."

"This must be a very hard time for you, Christina; losing your case and all."

"It is devastating. I feel gutted."

"Here in my hand is a leaked email from your lawyer to you and I hope you don't mind if I read this to our audience.

"And don't you worry, dear, you can't let this devastating set back destroy your confidence in yourself or your future," Dianne replied.

Email message to Christina Watson from Muni Bugden (Attorney at Law):
Confidential
December 26th, 2030
Dear Christina:

I wanted to let you know from me. Your case has been decided in favor of Bots R Us. Judge Bell ruled that this case has been going on for way too long, according to the judge; our request to postpone the hearing day appeared to only serve to anger the judge. Settlement hearing is scheduled for July 6th 2031. I am so sorry I can't represent you. This case has taken every penny that I have and I can't finance our Pro Bono arrangement any more. I am so sorry Christina.

With kind regards,
Muni Bugden (Attorney at Law).

Email message to Muni Bugden (Attorney at Law): Confidential

December 26th, 2030

Dear Muni:

I know you did your best. It went on for ten years. I feel so devastated. I haven't just lost Mathew and the case, my freedom and possibly body organs which are deemed unnecessary to maintain life, I have lost my faith in the system. And that for me is my biggest loss.

Regards Christina Watson

"I was going to say that I rather you didn't read my confidential email and actually I do mind. That email to my lawyer was supposed to be privileged and private."

"Christina, I am sorry, is too late; your most inner thoughts about this case have been broadcasted around the world. Is there anything you would like to add?"

"No."

Thank you loyal viewers for joining us, as we follow moment to moment in related matters concerning Pitville Disaster of 2030.

Chapter 18

December 26th 2030, around 9:00 p.m.

"Jackson," Dianne whispered as she focussed her eyes as carefully as she could while trying to keep her binoculars steady. "Do you see what I see?"

"Well let me see," Jackson said as Dianne placed the binoculars in front of Jackson's eyes.

"You are wiggling."

"Sorry."

"I can't believe it. It looks like pot plants are being burning inside a pretty primitive greenhouse setup. Imagine if all that smoke goes up, wonder what it will be like when that hell-hole Pitville smells and breathes all this?"

Dianne tried not to laugh. "Jackson this is serious, get as many shots as you can. Make some long shots and some zoomed in.

"Yes, boss, we are live."

"Welcome viewers. This is Dianne Black reporting live on location. As you can see, we are broadcasting live from the beautiful, but smoky skies above the Stonely Mountain fire. We at PPZ are asking questions, but we are not getting all the answers that we would like. There is always something we don't know and we at the PPZ, and especially me, believe that the public should know details of public policy. We are on our way to Pitville's Alternative Radio Station and we will cover the Stonely Mountain fire which is growing while we fly by. From what we are able to observe from the smoky sky, there is no visible effort of a fire suppression service that we can see.

With us today is one of my favorite Pitville personalities, and I know he is also one of yours too; I am pleased to re-introduce to you, Doctor Smith.

"Welcome Doctor Smith

"I know this mountain fire is beyond your expertise, but you certainly can tell us how this smoke will be affecting the public's health."

"First though, just for fun, how do you think this fire started?

"I really don't know. My guess is as good as anyone's. I am willing to guess that the fire on the mountain though is sharing either the same or interconnected coal seams as the fires we are seeing under the sidewalks in Pitville do," Doctor Smith replied.

"How could such a thing happen?"

"If a disaster is going to happen it will happen in Pitville," Jackson said spontaneously.

"Shh Jackson, I am asking Doctor Smith."

"As you can see this fire is spreading at an alarming rate. There are theories. I hope that any investigation includes an enquiry to why trash was being burned on top of a coal seam at the Buzzard Creek garbage dump, which has been the main location for burning Coalton Valley's trash, for over a hundred years."

"The glow of the fire is quite beautiful," Jackson observed as he tried to hold his camera steady while the helicopter was hovering about.

"Viewers, as we hover above these trees, using our artificial light source, we cannot be amazed at the numerous species of wild life which make their homes in the tree tops covering the lower region on the Eastside of the beautiful Beartut Mountain Range.

"Let I remind you, that Coalton Valley was once a beautiful place and had plenty of salmon. The Glacier has shrunk over the years, but when I was a boy, that glacier was iconic."

"Could we please get back to the pressing question, how do you think this fire started?"

"I have no idea," Doctor Smith replied. "Technically the coal seam could have been ignited either naturally or through another source. The source could be lighting or something as simple as careless smoking."

"As you can see viewers, below us appears to be extensive damage to a primitive greenhouse which is storing what appears to be thousands of very tall and thick plants. We will let you, the viewer decide what kind of plants they appear to be. According to our map, the greenhouse is on Federal land and it is not clear who owns the greenhouse. My word, I had no idea such an operation could be going on so close to civilization."

"Civilization? Those people on Stonely Mountain are not allowed to benefit from our sophisticated fire suppression services. At the same time, the militia and military are building walls that are antagonizing Ginger Goodwin's supporters. Members of G.O.D. are demonizing those who are climbing the wall, while tens of thousands of people are peacefully standing by the wall. Some of those people might be quietly praying for a miracle, and the life as we know it to return. I fear our way of life might be gone for ever. Ginger Goodwin, is now on the run while suffering from a serious lung condition; still willing to die for what he believes in."

"Well what about Tut Island's security. The draft is used to acquire men to fight the enemy so that Tut Island is protected from illegal miners who are steeling pillars from under the ground and causing infrastructure on the surface to collapse."

"Yes, but the key words here are able bodied men. Ginger is technically very ill which is a fact being ignored by members of G.O.D. With all that said, it is obvious that Ginger does not see the Minese workers as his enemy because they risked their own lives to save his life."

"Does Mr. Goodwin see the authorities as his enemy?"

"I suppose it depends on what the members of G.O.D. do to him next.

Dianne asked while Jackson was shaking his head while Christina was beginning to feel cramps of agony that she had never experienced before."

"I can't speak for Ginger, obviously. From my point of view, the ruling class are not that expert at things. They hire experts. Historically the ruling class hired servants to dress them and feed them. Authority is a subjective word. Expertise on the other hand is measurable."

"Now, to answer your question about the effects this mountain fire will have on public health. Theoretically, when combining the health risks with the coal dust that is usually in the air, and the extra pollution caused by all the recent explosions, I would advise anyone who has chest related issues or weakness to stay indoors, or better yet, find a way out of Pitville.

"Thank You so much Doctor Smith now back to you Steve."

"Thank you Dianne."

"Don't go away viewers. We still have more news to share. Ginger Goodwin is believed to be at Pitville Radio Station at this time and we are taking his beautiful partner to see him, which will be the first since his bizarre rescue which I still find unbelievable. Yes, viewers there were ten illegal immigrant miners and four of Ginger's mates from his morning crew, supported by borrowed emergency equipment, who found Mr. Goodwin in Section E's rescue chamber. He was carried through a maze of tunnels and led to freedom through an undisclosed exit.

Mr. Goodwin's four mates are still missing and are under investigation for unauthorized use of Coaltonstone Mine equipment, which I and my colleagues believe is unfair and very callous indeed.

Understandably, Mr. Goodwin's lung condition has worsened. Our moles tell us that Mr. Goodwin complained the whole time he was being carried to an undisclosed exit of the very complicated and undocumented tunnel system which lies under Coalton Valley that he could walk. Our moles tell us the two secret service bots that were accompanying Mr. Goodwin, and this situation is also under investigation, were left in Section E's safety chamber. Our moles tell us that Mr. Goodwin spent most of his time reading 'The Rights Of Man' to them.

Christina Watson is soldiering on and is sitting behind us as we speak. Christina is not feeling very well, but we can report that she did tell us how excited she is to see Ginger. We at PPZ are more than happy to facilitate this meeting. This will be first meeting since the first terrible explosion which occurred around 5:20 AM Sunday morning. Christina has been waiting for Ginger all that time.

My mole has also told me that Ginger Goodwin's A1 status is now non-negotiable even though only hours before he had been automatically classified as 4F due to his chronic lung condition which is documented in his personal medical records. Back to you Steve."

"Are we off the air now?" Doctor Smith asked.

"Yes we are," Dianne replied.

"Jackson I still need to talk to you about something in private, you know it is very important that…

"Look, I am trying to hear what Steve is saying. Please Doctor Smith, the other thing will have to wait."

"As you can see, Dianne, the cadets from Pitville Military Academy are involved in two jobs. They are helping the militia build the war around the security fence which is around Coaltonstone Mines' Administration building, but they are also monitoring, and sometimes pushing people who are climbing the wall. Some of these people actually appear to have climbing ropes and long spiked shoes, which appears to be serving two purposes. The shoes are facilitating the climbing of the wall, and they are also turning out to be dangerous when used as a weapon. Things are getting nasty around here that is for sure. Hold on, there seems to be a very young man flyking over the walls, wearing a camera, wanting to know his mother, Christina Watson is. He has gotten over the fence and has been allowed into the administration building.

"Oh my God," Christina said."

"Dianne, we need to do something, Christina has gone into shock and she is about to deliver her baby."

"Pilot, fly us to Pitville General Hospital as fast as you can. Christina is going into labor."

Chapter 19

December 26th 2030, around 10:00 p.m.

Welcome to Pitville alternative radio Station. We are located on Stonely Mountain and have a beautiful view. With us today is Ginger Goodwin; that is thee Ginger Goodwin, the one who escaped from Mine Five with the help of four members of his morning crew, and about a dozen illegal immigrant miners.

"First of all I want to say how wonderful it is to see you in person Ginger. And congratulations; children are such a blessing. I really don't know where to start."

"Well, let me start. I am against this war on the Minese on Tut Island. And I am against the Exclusion League. The question here is not borders, the miners who I met were decent men, and risked their lives and freedom to help save my life. They carried me all the way from the safety chamber in section E, through a maze of tunnels that I did not even exist. And they did that not because they were being paid or were receiving in personal gain, they helped me, because I was a man in need. They stood by me, and carried me until I saw daylight. These so called illegal immigrant workers are doing a job no one wants to do."

"Regardless of the ethics behind our economic conditions which I agree is never fair, doing the thing which feels right and natural should be our choice. The mega rich seem to be getting wealthier while the poor get poorer, don't you agree that is just the way things are and you have to accept them, Ginger?"

"Of course I don't agree. I believe there are times sharing ownership of production and working at a safer pace would shape a better world. The problems we are faced with today were created over a hundred years ago. The undocumented mines are hiring undocumented workers, but those undocumented mines were left here as a legacy of those who were here before us. A hundred years ago, when mine owners avoided bureaucracy and filing fees, many mines were left undocumented and abandoned. Today, when undocumented mines are broken into and the anthracite pillars are stolen, whoever is above that area and beyond is placed at serious risk."

"So, Mr. Goodwin, are you in favor of A.B. Peel and the Exclusion League members who back him?"

"Of course not."

"Why not?"

"The question you should be asking is who will be excluded next? Who will be degraded by poverty, homelessness and nuisance fines which only serve to keep track of the most vulnerable? When I was alone in the Pit, I thought I was going to die. I thought they were going to leave me down there to die and I had never felt so excluded in my life. When I came back up, it was like I had been away, and I noticed a negativity that I never noticed before, but now looking back, I know it existed, but I just was not as aware of it, until I, in a way, became an outsider looking in. So the question is, who will be next to be excluded?"

"That is a very good question and will probably never be answered."

"I and my crew have slaved in the pits of Coaltonstone Mines for over fifteen years. We have worked under conditions that were almost as bad as the conditions the illegal immigrant miners face. The difference is, we work in mines which are documented and have a minimal amount of transparency. The Minese work in mines which are invisible. The difference between our conditions is only due to an accident of birth. My Minese miner brothers are being forced to work in mines which are invisible to the general public and when they die, they are left in those mines to rot. Members of G.O.D. and the Exclusion League are forcing the draft onto us as and forcing us to fight for them, as if the ruling class were on our side, instead of our exploiters. They don't care if we are killed or disabled with lung disease while we work in their hell hole mines. If A.B. Peel and his Exclusion League backers have their way, they will inadvertently expand the beggar class, because in the end that is what exclusion does to people."

"So, Ginger, are you saying that you feel closer to the Minese Workers than you do to the members of G.O.D.?"

"I certainly do. I waited for three days, my air was almost gone, I was coughing and I really did think I was going to die. And who did I see coming out of nowhere, Sam, Kevin, Jay and George and ten Minese Miners who risked their lives and what little freedom they have, to rescue me. They rescued me, when the members of G.O.D. refused to let the rescue team go into Mine Five to rescue me, because it was too risky and expensive . And as my grandfather worked himself to death, no one helped him. So why wouldn't feel just as close to these illegal immigrant miners than I do to the members of G.O.D. who have drafted me to kill my miner brothers?

"I always find it strange that my poorest friends are the ones who are called for active service and my richest friends have never been called."

"Why should I turn on my miner brothers after they risked their lives to save my life?

"The authorities are calling you a draft dodger, a dodger of duty? How do you feel about that?"

"Really, they are calling me a dodger of duty. I am suffering from a lung disease since I have been exposed to mine dust since I was fifteen years old, and I was at one time documented as unfit for military duty. Why should someone who has bone spurs in his heels be exempt from military duty, but someone with a lung disease be forced to fight? This is just another example where politics does not make sense and only benefits one side, or one class of people, at the expense of the other side or class. And my point is that I am in the same class as my Minese miner brothers, and the ruling class does not care if I live or die. This was demonstrated during the reckless endangerment me and my morning crew experienced in Mine Five."

"What do you say to those who call you a coward?"

"Try putting the time I put in trapped in the pit. The only thing that saved me from going mad was the literature that I found.

The rights of man was inspiring to me, it showed how common sense makes us intelligent. Without being allowed to think we are not just in chains like some of the miners I saw in the tunnels underneath us, we have had our humanity compromised".

"Ginger Goodwin, will you be honest with me. Are you Deep Coal?"

"I sat there for three days in deep coal waiting to be rescued and my grandfather, the only man besides my morning crew and the Minese, died trying to get someone to move. I was totally isolated from the surface, just the way the minese I saw in the tunnels were, how could I possibly have been Deep Coal. It defies common sense."

"So the answer is no."

"Yes the answer is no."

"So, what now?"

"I would rather die than kill my miner brothers, no matter what color their skin happens to be. I would rather die than to have my humanity compromised. The team had to wait for the members of G.O.D. to authorize the mission, and those members were waiting for the perfect time for me to be rescued. They actually let George Coaltonstone seal Mine Five while I was still trapped. Now who would you feel you had a duty to serve and protect; the men who actually rescued me, or the men who were waiting for the perfect time to rescue me. If conditions had been perfect, there would have never been an explosion to start with and then I would have never been trapped. Of course the conditions in Mine Five are dangerous. Then when I reached the surface, I was treated like a criminal. I was not only accused of being Deep Coal, whatever that is, I was also found to be guilty just because I was being accused.

"Oh my God they are banging down the door."

"What?"

"Get out of here. Run, Ginger, run."

Chapter 20

December 27th 2030, around 7:00 a.m.

"Hello viewers. So much has happened. And it has happened so fast. Ginger Goodwin has been shot. John Bell is accused of shooting him, the city hall is on fire. And the fire is being called suspicious by the volunteer fire department. There isn't any fire repression service on Stonely Mountain. The Stonely Mountain taxpayers voted against having a separate fire suppression service, and Pitville taxpayers do not consider themselves to be part of the mountain community taxpayers association. So Pitville public policy on this matter, transmitted through a press release to us by the members of G.O.D., is to let the mountain fire burn, unless and only unless, human life is in danger.

In other Pitville Mine Disaster news, Christina Watson, Ginger Goodwin's partner, has delivered a very premature baby boy. The policy at Tut General Hospital is to not offer intensive care to premature babies with a gestation of twenty-two weeks and six days or less. The policy is to allow the babies to die of natural causes without interference. James Coaltonstone has been rumored to have taken the baby to an undisclosed location. The walk-in Pitville clinic is now closed until further notice. Both Doctor Smith and Doctor Knight are possibly at an unknown location looking after Christina and Ginger's baby. James Coaltonstone has also paid all debt Christina Watson owes Bots R Us, when she lost her civil case, which was to compensate her for the loss of her husband Mathew Watson. This case has been in the courts for over ten years, and has accumulated a hefty legal bill for Bots R Us. The fact that the case had been in the courts for so long worked in favor of Bots R The time delay certainly did not benefit Christina Watson who is now reported to be in a fragile state.

"We at PPZ draw opinions from many sources, and today we would like to introduce and welcome Doctor Janice Bell."

"Thank you, Dianne."

"I know I have been reporting one tragic event after another, and usually a birth is wonderful news. So what can you tell us about these very premature births? Could you begin telling Black Times' viewers why Pitville General Hospital doesn't treat premature babies with a gestation period of twenty-two weeks and six days or less?"

"Dianne, it is incorrect that we do not treat such undeveloped babies. We want all of our patients to be comfortable, no matter how small they may be."

"My mole informed me that James Coaltonstone bought his own life support mobile unit, and is keeping the baby alive, and he is doing quite well considering the circumstances."

"Please Dianne; you are interrupting my train of thought. I just forgot what I was about to say."

"We, at Black Times must report all the news. In this case, for the wealthiest man on Tut Island to buy such a unit for this little boy, is not only news worthy, it is in my opinion, a wonderful heartwarming story."

"Everyone has a right to their opinion on this emotional issue. You do know that Mr. Coaltonstone actually took our equipment and then gave us payment for it. We did accept the payment and his generous donation to our hospital, but we at Tut General Hospital cannot condone such disruptive behavior."

"Thank you for telling us all the details in regards to how Mr. Coaltonstone acquired the new baby's life support equipment. Without this equipment, the baby would have died, isn't that right, Doctor Bell?"

"We at Tut General Hospital see how these babies struggle. Such premature babies can only survive when given extreme intensive care."

"How can a member of the public get this equipment fast enough to save their baby, if they choose to do so?"

"I don't know if there is a way, unless you take our equipment the way Mr. Coaltonstone did. And if anyone pulls a stunt like that again, we at Pitville General Hospital will certainly be pressing charges."

"And what will you do with the babies? Throw them out on the floor?"

"Certainly not; we have an appropriate place for these preemies to rest."

"You mean to die?"

"We at Pitville General Hospital do not believe it is right to burden families and society as a whole with the complications such premature births present. The expense to offer every premature baby with a gestation period of twenty-two weeks and six days could bankrupt our medical system. Extreme premature babies cannot live without intensive medical intervention, so we have made a policy at Pitville General Hospital to only offer life support to babies who are born after twenty-four weeks of gestation and onwards, but not for babies who are born after only twenty-two weeks and six days or less of gestation. Do I make myself clear Dianne?"

"Certainly, Doctor Bell; back to you Steve."

"Is that it, my interview is over? It is not only Pitville General Hospital which has this policy; the bioethics committee for G.O.D. has given all medical practitioners the very same directive."

"Thank you once again Doctor Bell. I must follow Steve's report, so please excuse me."

"Hello everyone, we have more ground breaking news to report on our show, Black Times. The fire on Stonely Mountain is growing and it is about to engulf the Alternative Radio Station, Volunteers have hiked and flyked up to the mountain, some are ignoring orders to let the radio station burn, and some of the hikers are being arrested. Feelings are also being flamed at this moment due to reports that Pitville's hero Ginger Goodwin has been shot, though his body has been left in a disclosed area. We also have, what is now just a rumor that James Coaltonstone has married Christina Watson possibly around the time Ginger was shot though we do not know for sure. What we do know is that the Justice of the Peace and his wife, and adult son and daughter were woken up at 5:00 AM and performed a civil union, and the debt owing to Bots R Us has been paid in full. Christina Watson is free and she won't be forced to sell any of her unnecessary organs to help pay for her debt in a timely fashion.

"Now for the weather. We have very smoky skies above Pitville, so to all of you holiday flykers, caution is advised. And for those with respiratory issues there is an air advisory still in progress."

Chapter 21

December 28th 2030, around 9:00 a.m.

Welcome viewers Black Times, on location at the Pitville Mine Disaster of 20130.

Jackson, my loyal camera man was filming what appeared to be more smoke coming out of the road. As we were discussing whether it was possible that the smoke was a sign that one or several coal seams underground may be on fire, the road dangerously close to the right side of our car opened up without any warning. I am still shaking as you can see. It is hard to know what to report first. The Pitville Mining disaster is not just one event, as you can see; it is one thing after another. We are also discovering that many of the Pitville miners are suffering from black lung and were never told or treated for it. Apparently the miners were warned that if they sought medical attention for any lung problems they would lose their jobs and their related medical insurance coverage.

Another story we are following is the series of explosions that were detonated fairly close to Eagle Claw beach.

It is not our job at PPZ to speculate actual causes to all of these dangerous events, we usually invite experts to voice their opinions. Unfortunately no one from G.O.D returned our phone calls.

Many of our loyal listeners have voiced concerns that the recent explosions may have been experimental and possibly the actual source of an unexplained Bird-Flu like virus which closed both Coalton Elementary and Pitville High schools for three days, sending after around two hundred students had severe vomiting.

Chapter 22

December 28th 2030, around 10:00 a.m.

"Don't look out of the window Christina," James instructed.
"Why can't I?"

"Because everything looks so poor. Poverty can be mind-numbing and has no future. You see all those gates, all those broken dreams. The force of nature built all this and man's nature always seems divided."

"I want to see all that I am leaving behind and I want to see where I am going." Christina said; disgusted by Coaltonstone's greying facial stubble and stale tobacco smelling breath.

"You mustn't think that way, Christina. Don't feel like you are leaving your life behind, feel like you are moving into a new world. Once we reach the North Lands you will see how wonderful it is. Imagine building a technology to warm and melt some of the Arctic. It will be another one of my great dreams coming to life. Just wait until summer, you will see for yourself how wonderful the White Nights are. I love White Nights. You must remember that we have a life waiting for us, which will be even better than the life we left behind. We have little James…"

"I would rather you call him Ginger," Christina said.

"Ginger lived in his own little world, where love and kindness could overrule weapons of war. So now he is on the grave yard shift…

"Please, call the baby Ginger, and he is not your son, he is your grandson."

"Actually you are wrong. He is legally my son now; you signed the papers which make him legally my son along with the marriage license agreement which makes you my wife. We are all Coaltonstones now. To succeed in life, Christina we must compromise. Ginger is gone. You are now Mrs. Coaltonstone. Wealth is like a wall."

"You mean like that wall you kept building around the security fence of the Administration building, antagonizing peaceful protestors until they grew so angry they climbed it."

"Well not exactly. And that is not how I see it."

"Well it is the way I was forced to see the situation as I waited for three days, watching the crowds grow, waiting for Ginger to be rescued by his own people, who at the end did nothing, but break Ginger's granddaddy heart. No wonder he died so suddenly."

"Christina, you know life has limits and limits are different for different people. Not everyone can live on our side of the wall and if they did there would be far less for us to share. We have left the south behind the wall and the future is in the North. And if we wanted to we could put a no entry sign in every little shop which gets in the way of progress."

"Can you do that?"

"The Question is dear, what can they do? That is always the question. We will build high speed highways which lead to my golf courses, selling my wine, my beef, my beer. My name will be on all the labels. I will build the tallest of towers and I will be remembered for my achievements forever. I will be feared for my power will affect everything. Monuments made by me to feed my wealth will have a place in every major city on this God fearing Earth."

"You only feel this way because you lost the nomination to A.B. Peel. The Exclusion League delegates would have never nominated you. The Exclusion League went on about possible future court proceedings you could be involved in and then stacked all the cards against you. Your chances to be the commander of chief to G.O.D. have been destroyed."

"No, my dear, I don't feel this way; I am this way."

"What about us?"

"I have a beautiful honeymoon planned for us. We will be cruising around the Northern passage and then we will be welcomed by the highest of military officials on the other side of the Bering Strait where only very few are given permission to enter."

"Will we be able to leave there when we want?

"Of course we will be able to leave! Why do people throw out their refrigerators and old trucks anywhere that is convenient? Look at that mess. Everywhere you look, all you see is old and decrepit appliances and cars. It is nice to leave the war zone; despite all this garbage the country side seems more beautiful the further north we go," James said trying to sound pleasant.

"Christina stared out of the window feeling sick to her stomach.

"A bit of Champaign will make you feel better Christina, we are safe now. The crew are on our side, our capital keeps the beast at bay, you understand that don't you Christina."

"I miss my life, this is your life."

"No, this is our life, now."

"I could say that your old life was lost once you lost your case."

"No, my old life was lost when Ginger was shot."

"Are you sure this bridge is safe?"

"You doubt this miracle of modern technology?"

"I am just getting a terrible feeling. The ride feels shaky."

"Well these long bridges often feel that way."

"I feel terrible not being with the baby. And I am surprised we weren't arrested when you took one of their mobile life support systems. That was really something."

"I did convince them to take my money. I always do, you know. He is a cute little guy. All head. We will see him soon. Our doctors tell me he is fighting for life and there is nothing wrong in that. He will grow up to be a fighter that is for sure."

"He is so small and vulnerable. I feel guilty keeping alive and I would feel even guiltier letting him die."

"The doctors are there with him. If kangaroos can survive out of the mother's womb why can't humans?"

Christina stared at James in disbelief.

"The matter has been settled. Your life is always better when you are with me. Baby James cannot live without me. I am providing him with the latest technology and he is going to live because of me. We are going to have a great life and you will learn to love me. That is how arranged marriages work. A room is set up for Baby James and I was able to convince your doctors to meet us there, since they owe me a big favor, they were glad to set things up while I settle a few details with Ono."

"Settle what things?"

"This shipment is very valuable."

"Have you heard anything from the doctors yet?"

"Yes, he is just fine."

"How can he be fine if he is so small?"

"It will take a while, but he will be just fine."

"Keeping a baby that small on life support is purely experimental you know, James."

"Not exactly; they do it all the time in Mina. We have been stuck in Pitville for way too long. Anyway life is always experimental. That is how you move on from life's tumbles. You get up and do what you can to exist and survive. And Baby James is a little fighter. The doctors all agree. Doctor Knight and Doctor Smith will remain with us until Baby James doesn't need such intensive care anymore. Oh please don't look like you hate me, I am giving you a chance to keep your son alive.

"You know I am incredibly grateful for the things you have been able to do for us, but sometimes I wonder if we would have been better off if all these horrible mishaps had been prevented."

"Baby James will grow and learn and see the world in a special way and if he survives, he will be stronger than any of us who have had it softer, will ever be."

"What happens if he is blind, deaf, or has heart problems?"

"He won't be. He will beat the odds. He is a Coaltonstone. Christina, it won't take long to feel at home on our ship. We will work on our second book, which could be just as popular as 'The Blessing: Black Diamonds' and you will learn to be happy with me. This was a similar arrangement I had with the first Mrs. Coaltonstone. Maybe we could help find a cure for cancer. That would be great. We must live the lives fate presents us with and so

Baby James will learn to do the same. With everything that you might detest about me, you eat better, you dress better and you couldn't look more beautiful than when you are with me. I will take care of baby James as if he were my own, because he is part of you.

"And part of Ginger. I mean he is your grandson, so of course he is part of you too."

Chapter 23

December 29th 2030, around 10:00 a.m.

"Isn't this wonderful," James Coaltonstones said as his feet dangled from the ship into the cool water.

"The water is too cold for me," Christina said as she quickly stood up.

While putting on her shoes and socks, James said, baby James is in his special place and Doctor Knight is attending to his every need for the 12 hour day shift and Doctor Smith will be doing a 12 hour night shift."

"How did you manage to persuade them to close their clinic?"

"The same way I persuade everyone to do what I need done. It wasn't that hard to do. I explained to them, we as a crew, will be the first civilians to be allowed into the brand new tunnel connecting North America to Asia and Europe. This will be a similar journey taken by our ancestors two hundred thousand years ago, but only in the opposite direction. This Tunnel could change everything. We will be guests of the small military base on the other side where I will meet Ono. He is with the shipment, of coal, hemp and jade and I forget what else, some electronics I believe."

"Are you joking?"

"About what?"

"Don't look so glum. You are a Coaltonstone now which means positive thinking and a stiff upper lip."

"You are sounding like a member of the Royal Family.

"In a way I am. I have often been referred to as King Coal, but now that hemp and Boss-bots are in such demand, soon I will be referred to as King of Everything. The Jade we are exporting is just icing on our cake."

"You mean smuggling?"

"No, I mean exporting. You always make me sound so despicable. We are surviving and living a lot more than the folks we left behind. We are the winners. We won the race. I am providing everything James will need, and I am certain he will grow into a capable and strong man. He has already beaten some odds against him; just like I do. Baby James will be the son my other sons could never be. I don't know where I went wrong. I tried so hard to provide them with a life balance. Now I have one son in jail, and the other son refusing to speak to me.

"Christina, what is that?" It looks like a boy flyking. I didn't know that those suits had such a range."

"Oh my God it is Mathew."

"Your son Mathew?"

"Tell me son where did you get such a wonderful flyking suit? I just love all those feathers you have sown on to it."

"Actually Grandma helped. I collected the feathers and Grandma sewed them on for me. Then when I made ten thousand dollars selling photographs to a guy called Steve from the PPZ, I bought all these extra things. I sold some photographs and refitted my flyking suit into a new hybrid pipe model which recharges with the wind and sun."

"Isn't that amazing? He looks so much like his father, Christina. I always wanted you to know how sorry I was about the accident, but business is business. You know that. It is the way it must be. You know how members of G.O.D. have decimated the coal and steel industries. I wanted to bring them back to the way they used to be, but I lost. I wish I could bring Mathew back, but you lost. If I could make it all up to you I would, but business is business. Let us have lunch together, like a real family.

"Mom, I found you. I thought I would never see you again."

Mathew landed on the deck, and before he was able to turn off his suit he was being hugged by a tearful Christina.

"Mom, I want to see my new brother, I want to be with you. Grandma said that I had to accept the way things are. Ginger never would do that why should I?

"Hello Son. We were just about to have lunch in Baby James' special room.

"Baby James? His name is Ginger. Right Mom?

"Why are you calling him Baby James? His name is Ginger; right Mom?

"We can talk about this later, Mathew. Now when you see your brother, make sure you are very quiet and careful. And you have to stand behind glass until he gets stronger.

"Why?"

"Your brother is very tiny and very weak. He is the size of a twenty-one week old fetus and he cannot fight germs the way you and I can."

"Why?"

"Because your brother is very tiny and very weak. He is the size of a twenty-two week old fetus."

"I thought he was a baby."

"Well he is a baby. I meant that your brother is at the same developmental age as a twenty-one week old fetus. Now thank your Uncle James for helping us. I would still be in Debtor Prison if it hadn't been for him, and your baby brother would not be alive if it wasn't for your Uncle James. You like Doctors Knight and Smith, right? They are here too. They work separately in twelve hour shifts, so baby James will have 24 hour care.

"What would you like for lunch Mathew?"

"I would like ice cream."

"Ice cream it shall be."

"James, Mathew will be having what we are having. First will be lobster soup. Then we were going to have salmon and rice, then and only then we will have ice cream."

"Okay, you are the boss dear."

"Why did you just call my Mom dear? What is going on?"

"We are married. Your mom and your baby brother James are Coaltonstones."

"Why?"

"Son, not every young man gets to enjoy a luxury cruise owned by his new step dad."

"I won't have to call him Dad, will I Mom?"

"Of course not. You can continue calling me Uncle James, like you always have," James Coaltonstone said as he tried to hug Mathew while he was pulling away.

"Mom, I want to go home."

"Mathew, please. You must act mature now. We are going to a new life. Your old life is gone."

"You mean like Ginger? Are we all going to get shot?"

"Of course not, Mathew," Christina replied.

"It is horrible in Pitville now. I flyked over the wall to see if I could find you; everyone told me you were gone, and Grandma was crying. And all these armed men were either guarding or building a wall around the security fence. And you wouldn't believe what I saw in between the two walls? Then Steve from PPZ came up to me and said that I was the first to flyke over the wall and then he noticed my helmet camcorder. He asked me if it was on. I said yes. And he bought the photographs and my memory card. I have two more memory cards though."

"I know what lies between those two walls; I am the one who authorized John Bell's designs. What you know is classified and we need to talk about this later. Now on to lunch and before you meet your little brother remember that he is very frail, a miracle of my generosity."

"Uncle James is saving your brother's life. The hospital has a rule so we had to take the baby home."

"Damn those G.O.D. members, they write all their rules in stone."

"James, please, they are the Government's Official Directors and they do a lot of good work."

"They are always watching. They don't respect privacy or private property the way we do. They would have watched Baby James die without ever having a chance to live; while we the taxpayer pay them to write a report."

"Why are we calling the baby James, I thought his name was Ginger?" Mathew asked.

"Well, we can call him both dear, isn't that right, James."

"Certainly. Ginger James sounds grand, doesn't it?" James Coaltonstone said, agreeably.

"Why was he born so fast? Was it so we could share birthdays together for as long as we live?"

"Maybe, dear."

Chapter 24:

December 29th 2030, around 10:00 p.m.

"Christina where are you going? Christina answer me! Christina don't. Oh Christina. Stop the ship. Someone help me please."

"Mom! Someone help my mom please, will someone help my mom.

The crew on hand pulled Christina out of the frigid cold water and she was soon on life support, lying beside her baby Ginger.

Doctor Knight read the quick text Christina had written before she fell from the ship or jumped off. No one knew for sure.

Hi Doctor Knight:

Well here I am in a terrible state. I am Mrs. James Coaltonstone. The Justice of the peace was phoned early in the morning hours after Ginger was shot, and the baby was born and it was also Mathew's fourteenth birthday. The Justice of the Peace was at home, we married at his house, his wife and his two adult sons were witnesses. I told James Coaltonstone that I loved Ginger and he told me only as a family could we save baby Ginger James. I made sure that I kept my poker face on so he couldn't tell how much I hated the whole idea. He said now that I am Mrs. James Coaltonstone I am too rich to harass or hurt in any way.

I know now it is impossible to fight the system and I can hear Ginger calling me.

I want a better life for Mathew Junior and Ginger Junior That is why I allowed James to change their names. We are spending our honeymoon speculating on how James can use dam technology to warm the Arctic Ocean to free the wealth frozen under the virgin north, the New Frontier for him and all of his labels.

THE END

Produced by S.E. McKenzie Productions
First Print Edition March 2016

Enquiries: 1(778)992-2453
Mailing Address:
S. E. McKenzie Productions
168 B 5th St.
Courtenay, BC
V9N 1J4

Email Address:
messidartha@aol.com

http://www.amazon.com/SarahMcKenzie/e/B00H9RWX48/

www.ingramcontent.com/pod-product-compliance
Lightning Source LLC
Chambersburg PA
CBHW070642130626
46555CB00006B/2663